This Book Belongs To

Thank you for your purchase

First edition: June 2023

Designed by: RV AppStudios Team

Contact us: www.rvappstudios.com

ISBN: 9781960790101

LUCAS'S ADVENTURE TO THE SHED

Settle into bed, my dear. I have a story for you.
One that's sweet and funny and kind and magical and new.

For when you fall asleep tonight, all cuddled in your bed.
My wish for you is that you have this story in your head.

A smile on your little face and a song inside your heart.
Stories are the thing of dreams, and now it's time to start.

Lucas and Ruby were best friends who loved playing. They loved using their imaginations and creating wonderful worlds around them. Sharing their incredible adventures together was all they wanted to do. But sometimes, even great adventurers need to help with the chores.

Lucas's mom stepped onto the back porch and called her son inside.

"Mom," Lucas asked. "Is this going to take long? Ruby and I were right in the middle of figuring out how much peanut butter fits in my bike helmet."

"While that does sound very scientific and also extremely messy, I need you to clean out the shed," Lucas's mom answered.

Lucas did not look very happy but knew it was important to help around the house. He did have a great imagination and was sure he and Ruby could make cleaning the shed into a super fun adventure.

Lucas ran back outside and told Ruby about the change in plans. She set down his bike helmet, which was now overflowing with peanut butter, and gladly accepted the challenge.

"I'm happy to help. What's in your shed anyway?" Ruby asked.

Lucas got a wild look in his eyes, turned to Ruby, and said, "Only the greatest treasures the world has ever known!"

"Really?!" Ruby responded excitedly.

"Well, I mean I'm not totally sure, but I bet there's something cool in there," Lucas said as they walked toward the shed. "Whatever it is, I know that you and I will have a good time exploring."

"And cleaning," said Lucas's mom as she dropped a trash bag outside the shed.

"Yes, mom, cleaning and exploring," Lucas said with a wink.

Lucas and Ruby stood in front of the shed which, in a matter of seconds, transformed in their imaginations to a giant cave. They wore headlamps to light their way, and cave-exploring equipment filled a backpack that Lucas threw over his shoulder.

"Let's go," he said as they took their first steps into the shed... I mean a giant treasure-filled cave.

"I think I found something already!" called out Lucas as his voice echoed off the cave walls. "It's a giant strand of the most wonderful, sparkly gems and jewels in all the world!"

"Yes. And definitely not your dad's old garden hose," laughed Ruby.

"Let's stick to our imaginations," giggled Lucas. "Look at this sack full of gold nuggets and this magical unicorn!"

"Amazing! I just found four enormous solid silver plates. Maybe owned by a giant who used to live here," Ruby said, giving Lucas a quick glance.

"Or maybe the giant still lives here," Lucas said quietly.

Just then something fell from the cliff above their heads. As they looked up they saw... A GIANT! However, lucky for Lucas and Ruby, he was the sweetest and kindest giant ever.

He helped them clean... I mean, explore the rest of the cave for treasure. In no time, they had collected it all to bring to a museum and share with the world.

"Lucas, how's it going?" called out his mom as she walked toward the shed.

"That was one of our best adventures yet," Lucas said with a huge smile.

"Top three adventures this week for sure," Ruby added.

"Adventure? Cleaning the shed?" asked Lucas's mom in a funny tone. "Well, I'm glad you had fun and the shed got cleaned. But wait, I didn't know your dad was going to help you too."

At that moment, Lucas's dad walked out of the shed holding a full garbage bag.

"You know I couldn't pass up exploring a cave filled with the world's greatest treasurers," Lucas's dad said.

"Cave exploring? World's greatest treasurers? You mean your old garden hose and that deflated unicorn pool float?" Lucas's mom asked, sounding confused. "You know what, it sounds like it was a lot of fun. Maybe you can help me turn cleaning out your bike helmet into a great adventure."

"You mean that crater filled with prehistoric goo that may be filled with dinosaur fossils?" Lucas said with a smirk.

"Yes, that's the one," his mom giggled, as off they went on another great adventure.

Now off to Dreamland to begin a great night.
Filled with magic and wonder and glowing starlight.

You'll wake tomorrow with new stories and then.
You'll head back to Dreamland and do it again.

Educational Books for Kids

I LOVE YOU LUCAS
(Storybook)

ABC Tracing Workbook

NUMBER Tracing Book

ABC Coloring Book

LARGE ABC Letters,
Number & Shape Tracing

SCISSOR SKILLS
Preschool Activity Book

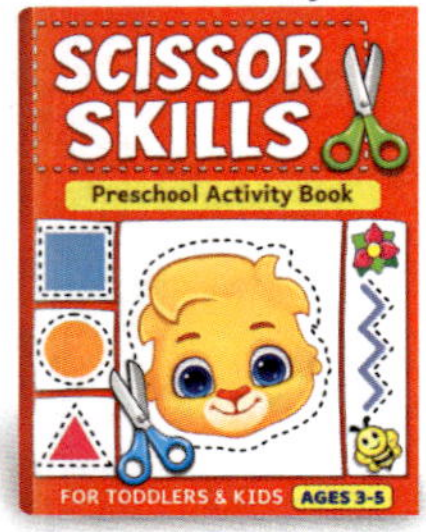

SIGHT WORDS
Book For Kids

COLORING BOOK
For Kids

PRESCHOOL MATH
Activity Book

CURSIVE
Handwriting Workbook

100 TIMED TESTS
Addition and Subtraction

KINDERGARTEN MATH
Activity Book

HOW TO DRAW
For Kids Ages 4-8

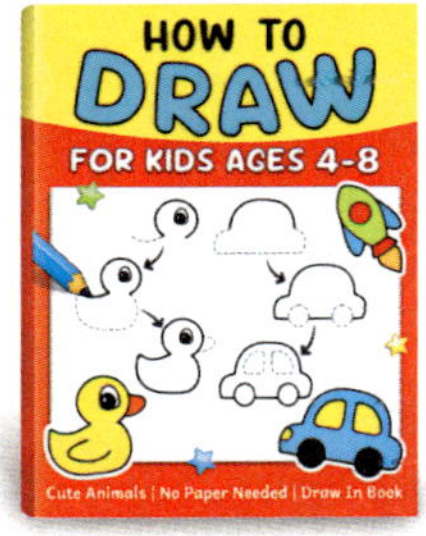

ABC Activity Book &
Alphabet Letter Tracing

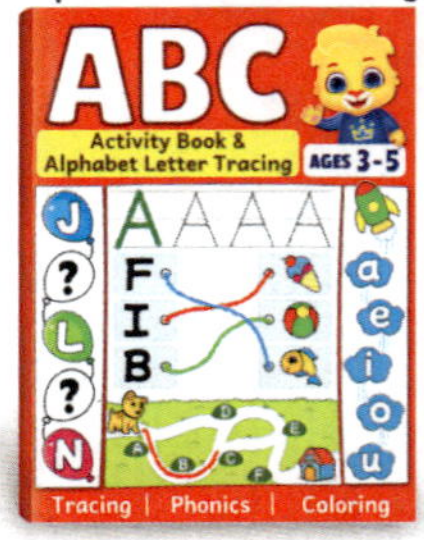

KINDERGARTEN
WRITING WORKBOOK

Kindergarten & 1st Grade
WRITING PAPER
With Blank Picture Space

NUMBER TRACING
Workbook For Kids

COLOR BY NUMBERS
COLORING BOOK FOR KIDS

WORD SEARCH
For Kids Puzzle Book

LUCAS & FRIENDS

Official Lucas & Friends Merch On Amazon

Our Impact

RV AppStudios is one of the largest mobile kids app developers in the world. Over 150 million kids will play with our apps this year, and that's for FREE and without ads.

Made in United States
North Haven, CT
05 August 2024

55770818R00022